CONTENTS

KU-760-834

Meet Bug Team Alpha 4

Chapter 1 7

Chapter 2 17

Chapter 3 27

Chapter 4 37

Chapter 5 47

Chapter 6 57

Chapter 7 67

Chapter 8 77

Chapter 9 87

Chapter 10 97

Mission report 106
Glossary 108
About the author 109
About the illustrator 109
Discussion questions 110
Writing prompts 111

Bug Team Alpha is the most elite Special Operations force of the Colonial Armed Forces of the Earth Colonial Coalition. Each member has an insect's DNA surgically grafted onto his or her human DNA. With special abilities and buglike features, these soldiers are trained to tackle the most dangerous and unique combat missions. Their home base is *Space Station Prime*.

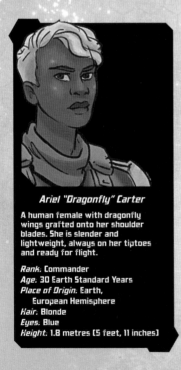

Ariel "Dragonfly" Carter

A human female with dragonfly wings grafted onto her shoulder blades. She is slender and lightweight, always on her tiptoes and ready for flight.

Rank: Commander
Age: 30 Earth Standard Years
Place of Origin: Earth,
    European Hemisphere
Hair: Blonde
Eyes: Blue
Height: 1.8 metres (5 feet, 11 inches)

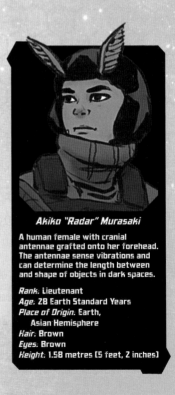

Akiko "Radar" Murasaki

A human female with cranial antennae grafted onto her forehead. The antennae sense vibrations and can determine the length between and shape of objects in dark spaces.

Rank: Lieutenant
Age: 28 Earth Standard Years
Place of Origin: Earth,
    Asian Hemisphere
Hair: Brown
Eyes: Brown
Height: 1.58 metres (5 feet, 2 inches)

SCI-FINITY

BUG TEAM ALPHA
THE DIG

by Laurie S Sutton
illustrated by James Nathaniel

15 396 999 X

Raintree is an imprint of Capstone Global Library Limited, a
company incorporated in England and Wales having its registered
office at 264 Banbury Road, Oxford, OX2 7DY – Registered
company number: 6695582

www.raintree.co.uk
myorders@raintree.co.uk

Text © Capstone Global Library Limited 2018
The moral rights of the proprietor have been asserted.

All rights reserved. No part of this publication may be reproduced
in any form or by any means (including photocopying or storing it
in any medium by electronic means and whether or not transiently
or incidentally to some other use of this publication) without the
written permission of the copyright owner, except in accordance
with the provisions of the Copyright, Designs and Patents Act
1988 or under the terms of a licence issued by the Copyright
Licensing Agency, Saffron House, 6–10 Kirby Street, London EC1N
8TS (www.cla.co.uk). Applications for the copyright owner's
written permission should be addressed to the publisher.

Edited by Abby Colich
Designed by Kyle Grenz
Production by Katy LaVigne

ISBN 978 1 4747 4908 4 (paperback)
20 19 18 17
10 9 8 7 6 5 4 3 2 1

British Library Cataloguing in Publication Data
A full catalogue record for this book is available from
the British Library.

Acknowledgements
We would like to thank the following for permission to reproduce
photographs: Shutterstock: Mihai-Bogdan Lazar, throughout
(starfield), Somchai Som, throughout (Earth); Design elements:
Capstone and Shutterstock

Every effort has been made to contact copyright holders of
material reproduced in this book. Any omissions will be rectified
in subsequent printings if notice is given to the publisher.

Printed and bound in China.

Liu "Hopper" Yu

A human male with grasshopper legs grafted onto his hips. Footpads take the place of footwear. He is slender and always springy, ready to jump.

Rank. Lieutenant
Age. 21 Earth Standard Years
Place of Origin. Earth,
   Asian Hemisphere
Hair. None, head is shaved
Eyes. Brown
Height. 1.88 metres (6 feet, 2 inches)

Irene "Impact" Mallory

A human female with a beetle exoskeleton grafted onto her body. She's always slightly hunched over, like a linebacker ready to charge an opponent.

Rank. Lieutenant
Age. 24 Earth Standard Years
Place of Origin. Earth,
   European Hemisphere
Hair. Brown
Eyes. Brown
Height. 1.68 metres (5 feet, 6 inches)

Gustav "Burrow" Von Braun

A human male with digger beetle arms grafted onto his torso. He is heavyset and very muscular.

Rank. Lieutenant
Age. 24 Earth Standard Years
Place of Origin. Earth,
   European Hemisphere
Hair. Brown
Eyes. Brown
Height. 1.68 metres (5 feet,
   6 inches)

Sancho "Locust" Castillo

A human male with wings and a dorsal exoskeleton grafted onto his body. He has immense strength and flying capabilities.

Rank. Lieutenant
Age. 23 Earth Standard Years
Place of Origin. Earth,
   South American Hemisphere
Hair. Light brown
Eyes. Brown
Height. 1.83 metres (6 feet)

CHAPTER 1

"Bug Team Alpha, deploy!" came the command.

"Bug Team Alpha!" was the response as the team surged forwards on foot, on vehicles and into the air.

"Impact! Take point and break through the front line of the enemy defence," Commander Ariel "Dragonfly" Carter ordered over the comm.

Lt Irene "Impact" Malloy ran on foot towards the mass of attacking grunt drones like an angry bull. She was as big as one too. Oncoming blaster fire stung like hail against her thick, beetlelike exoskeleton. She returned the favour with her pulse weapon set on scattershot mode for the widest coverage. Then Impact smashed into the drone line, using her carapace like a natural battering ram. Grunt drones fell before the onslaught.

"I'm through!" Impact reported.

"Burrow! Hopper! Radar! Go, go, go!" Commander Jackson "Vision" Boone instructed.

stav "Burrow" Von Braun sped on a Hover
rds the opening in the enemy line created by
He deployed the digging spikes on his arms and
legs, ready to sweep aside the enemy. Lt Akiko "Radar"
Murasaki rode on a smaller Bug Bike next to him. She
was too petite to drive a huge, heavy-duty Hover Hog,
but she had incredible fighting skills. Lt Liu "Hopper" Yu
bounced alongside both of them on long, grasshopper
DNA-enhanced legs. They made him very tall, and a
very visible target.

Blaster fire exploded around the three of them.
But Radar's ultrasensitive cranial antennae felt the
vibrations of the energy blasts the moment they were
fired. She interpreted the strength and direction and
warned her teammates. Burrow swerved his anti-gravity
megacycle to avoid hits. Hopper leaped up high and over
out of harm's way.

"Locust! It's a go for aerial assault!" Dragonfly
ordered.

Lt Sancho "Locust" Castillo buzzed through the
air using his sturdy insect wings. He flew point for a
squad of Buzzer helicopters carrying Colonial Armed
Forces troops into the battle. Using a single blaster, he

saturated the landing site with suppressive fire as the Buzzers delivered reinforcements. The enemy drones started to retreat. Bug Team Alpha pursued.

Suddenly, the battlefield disappeared from around the combatants. Bug Team Alpha stood in a Holo-Sim chamber on *Space Station Prime* in orbit above Earth.

"Training session is over," Vision announced from the Holo-Sim monitor room. "Well done, team. Dismissed."

The team left the combat simulator. Even though Bug Team Alpha was a Special Ops group of elite fighters, they practised every day in the Holo-Sim. That was only part of what kept them elite. They were extraordinary because of their insectlike appearance and abilities. Each member had a different insect's DNA surgically grafted onto his or her human DNA. It also gave each of them special powers.

In the monitor room, a call came in to Bug Team Alpha's commanding officers. The face of their superior officer appeared on the comm screen.

"General Barrett, sir!" Vision and Dragonfly said in unison.

"Commander Dragonfly, assemble a mission team. I have an assignment for you," the general said. "The briefing specs are being transmitted now."

"Yes, sir!" Commander Dragonfly replied as she synced her wrist computer to the incoming data. The general's image blinked off the monitor.

"And his reputation for brevity remains unchallenged," Vision observed. He gave his fellow officer a pat on the shoulder as he left the monitor room. "Good luck with the mission."

Commander Dragonfly stood up from her chair and stretched her dragonfly wings as she viewed the mission specs. Then she called up the dossier files for the entire membership of Bug Team Alpha. As she chose the individuals for this specific mission, she transferred their data onto her wrist computer.

— — — — — — — — —

Lt Liu "Hopper" Yu. Grasshopper DNA graft. Leaping ability. Age: 21 Earth Standard Years. Planet of origin: Earth, Asian Hemisphere.

— — — — — — — — —

Lt Akiko "Radar" Murasaki. Cranial Antennae DNA graft. Vibration detection. Age: 28 Earth Standard Years. Planet of origin: Earth, Asian Hemisphere.

Lt Irene "Impact" Mallory. Beetle Exoskeleton DNA graft. High-impact tolerance and strength. Age: 24 Earth Standard Years. Planet of origin: Earth, European Hemisphere.

Lt Gustav "Burrow" Von Braun. Digger beetle arm and leg spike DNA graft. Enhanced tunnelling abilities and strength. Age: 24 Earth Standard Years. Planet of origin: Earth, European Hemisphere.

Lt Sancho "Locust" Castillo. Locust DNA graft. Wings and dorsal exoskeleton. Heavy-duty flight and strength. Age: 23 Earth Standard Years. Planet of origin: Earth, South American Hemisphere.

Satisfied with her choices, Commander Dragonfly called her team to the briefing room.

A few minutes later, the selected team members settled into the plush, padded chairs. They all knew it was the last time in a while that they would sit somewhere so comfortable. Commander "Dragonfly" Carter stood at a podium and described their assignment.

"We've got a search and rescue," the commander began. "A team of archaeologists conducting an excavation on planet Niburi 3 dug up something dangerous. The camp has been attacked. One scientist, by the name of Dr Franks, is missing. The number of attackers is unknown. No direct sightings as of yet. Our mission is to find the missing person and neutralize the threat to the project. Any questions?"

"When do we leave?" Lt Hopper asked eagerly as he fidgeted his long, grasshopper legs.

"Departure is in 20," Commander Dragonfly replied. "Dismissed."

After 12 Earth Standard Hours, the Zip Ship *Arion* dropped out of hyperspace just outside the Niburi star system. The light-transport vessel confirmed coordinates and proceeded towards Niburi 3 – the third planet from the Sun. Aboard the ship were the six members of the Colonial Armed Forces Special Ops Bug Team Alpha.

From orbit the planet looked like a big brown ball. It was mostly dry tundra with patches of green forests scattered over the surface. There was water on the planet, but there were no oceans, no major rivers and no large lakes.

"Get ready to hit the dirt in 10!" Commander Dragonfly barked from the cockpit. "Full combat gear! Triple check weapons! Comm! Backups and emergency medical packs!"

"Ready!" Radar replied.

"Ready!" Impact shouted.

"Ready!"

"Ready!"

"Ready!"

Dragonfly nosed the ship into Niburi 3's atmosphere. It pierced through the thin upper cloud layers like a dagger. Halfway down to the planet's surface the *Arion* hit a thermal layer of unstable air that tossed the ship like a leaf in the wind. Commander Dragonfly had her hands full keeping the craft steady. When the *Arion* finally set down on the archaeological dig's designated landing site, Lt Radar threw up.

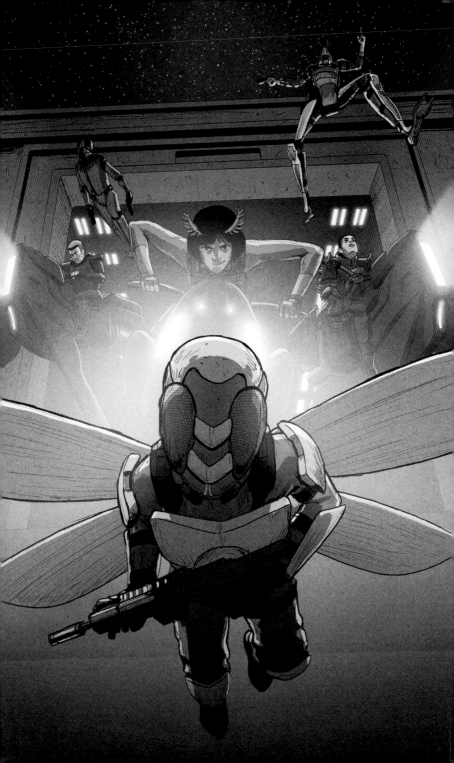

"Sorry. Too many hard vibes," she explained. "No offence, Commander."

"None taken. Bug Team Alpha – mobilize!" Dragonfly ordered as she punched the hatch release.

No one knew what to expect when they stepped out onto the dry, grassy planet. Bug Team Alpha knew only that they had been deployed for an emergency search and rescue.

"We're up against unidentified hostiles. Their numbers are unknown," Commander Dragonfly said as she activated her helmet comm, shouldered her blaster and then deployed her wings. She buzzed out of the ship ahead of her squad.

The team exited the ship in combat mode. Lt Hopper bounced clear of the hatch on his long legs. Radar zoomed down the ramp on a small Bug Bike. Impact and Burrow were too bulky for bikes, so they rode Hover Hogs. Lt Locust flew at the rear of the formation.

They aimed their weapons at the first thing they saw.

CHAPTER 2

"Stop! Don't shoot!" a small woman shouted as the team rushed towards her.

The woman had long black hair tied in a plait and wore a bright shirt with a pattern of large flowers. Her khaki shorts were covered in dust. A well-worn baseball cap shielded her head and face from the strong sunlight.

"I . . . I'm Dr Leialoha – director of this dig!"

"Hold fire!" Dragonfly ordered.

The team surrounded the woman. They took their fingers off their triggers but did not drop their aim. Lt Radar swivelled her antennae towards Leialoha.

"Radar! Scan her!" the commander said.

Lt Radar stepped forwards from the team's defensive formation and swivelled her buglike antennae towards Dr Leialoha.

"Her vibrations identify her as human. She's legit. Not a hostile," Lt Radar reported.

"At ease," Dragonfly told the team. They relaxed, but did not break formation.

"Um, thanks for coming," Dr Leialoha said.

"If there's trouble, we're there," Commander Dragonfly replied as she settled back onto the ground and folded her wings. "What's your status?"

"Dr Franks is still missing," Dr Leialoha explained. "But there haven't been any more attacks – so far. Everyone's nervous, though."

After the Bug Team members secured the *Arion*, Dr Leialoha climbed onto the back of Impact's Hover Hog and directed the team along a dirt path through a patch of woodland forest. It was one of the scattered areas of green they had seen from space.

"I don't hear any birds," Lt Impact noticed.

"I don't see any insects, either," Lt Locust observed. "Except for us."

"The planet is only now recovering from a devastating swarm of meteor strikes that turned it barren thousands of years ago," Dr Leialoha told them. "The ecosystem is coming back, but in some very unexpected ways. For example, there aren't any small birds or insects, but there are herds of large grazing animals. We still don't have a picture of the entire food chain."

"Is that what the dig is about?" Dragonfly asked.

"No, the dig is about that," Dr Leialoha replied as they came out of the forest. She pointed to a huge mound rising up out of a meadow. It was about three storeys high and shaped like an upside-down cone covered in brown grass. There were no other structures anywhere nearby. The sides were smooth and regular. It was obviously an artificial construction.

"It doesn't look like much," Hopper commented.

"It's bigger on the inside," Dr Leialoha assured him.

Suddenly, a tall, thin man in a medic's lab coat rushed towards Dr Leialoha and the Bug Team.

"Dr Barrington! What's wrong?" Dr Leialoha asked.

"We caught it! We have it!" Barrington gasped with excitement. His long brown hair was tied back in a ponytail, but much of it had come loose from his sprint. Like Leialoha, he wore a baseball cap in the bright sun.

"Caught what?" Commander Dragonfly asked sharply as she and the team tensed.

"The thing that attacked the camp!" Dr Barrington exclaimed. "We tranquilized it inside the dig!"

"Take us to it," the commander said.

Burrow pulled the medical doctor onto the back of his Hover Hog. The team sped to the project's camp at the base of the mound. It was made up of small, sturdy buildings constructed from steel and polycrete.

Dr Barrington guided the Bug Team to a compact structure designated as the Infirmary. They parked their vehicles and went inside. There they saw an unconscious creature strapped to an exam table.

"I don't think the Bug Team has ever seen anything like that before," Commander Dragonfly said.

"Yeah, and we've seen a lot," Lt Impact added.

The creature was humanoid but had scales instead of skin. Its legs and feet looked like a lizard's. It had no arms. Instead, snakelike tendrils covered the front and back of its torso. Its head was reptilian.

"It . . . it looks like the images that are painted on all the walls inside of the dig!" Dr Leialoha exclaimed.

"We believe that the paintings are of the planet's inhabitants from before the meteor strike disaster. We call them 'Medusas,' after the mythological Greek monster, because of the snakelike tendrils on their bodies."

"This creature can't have been alive all that time," Commander Dragonfly said.

"No. That's impossible," Dr Leialoha agreed. "But how can it be here now?"

Suddenly, another archaeologist rushed into the building. His clothes were covered in dirt and his skin was scratched.

"There's been another attack in the dig!" the man gasped.

"Dr Sutherland! Are you all right? Were you attacked?" Dr Leialoha asked.

"Not me. It's Dr Franks. I didn't see what got him. I fell trying to get out of the dig site," Dr Sutherland replied. Then he saw the xenoform on the table. His eyes grew wide. "What is that?"

"Wait a minute. Dr Franks? I thought he was already missing," Commander Dragonfly said.

"No, Dr Laurel Franks is missing. But now her husband, Dr Millerd Franks, has been attacked too," Leialoha clarified.

"Millerd Franks was attacked after you captured this Medusa. That means there's a second Medusa at large. Or more," Dragonfly concluded. "Dr Sutherland, show us where the attack occurred."

"I'm not going back in there!" he said. "Take my data chip."

Commander Dragonfly loaded the excavation data into her wrist computer. A schematic map was displayed.

"Millerd was in chamber 15," Dr Sutherland said.

"Please, don't hurt the Medusas," Dr Leialoha pleaded. "There's so much we can learn from them."

"They've presented a very clear danger to your personnel," Dragonfly reminded the archaeologist. "But I promise we will not attack unless under dire threat. Bug Team Alpha, is that clear? Now move out!" she stated before giving them a chance to answer.

*   *   *

The mound really was bigger on the inside. It was an underground pyramid with tight tunnels made from large stone blocks that sloped down into the ground and twisted like a maze. The map schematics kept the team on track. The only light came from their weapon scopes and a few lamps left by the archaeologists. Lt Radar's antennae twitched with every step.

"I'm not picking up any vibes," Radar reported. "But something sure stinks down here."

"Smells rotten," Burrow said.

"Like a grave," Hopper shuddered.

"Cool the chatter," Dragonfly ordered. She kept her wings folded in the tight corridor. "Stay focused."

The team reached chamber 15. It was in a mess. Dozens of tall pottery cylinders lay on their sides. Each was painted with images of the Medusas. One of the cylinders was broken open and empty.

"Can't tell if these tracks are old or new," Dragonfly said as she pointed her scope light at the confusion of boot prints in the dirt. "But one of them has to be Dr Franks'. Split into teams. Burrow and Locust. Impact and Radar. Hopper, you're with me."

Each team entered separate tunnels branching off chamber 15. They kept track of their positions with pings on their wrist computers.

Dragonfly and Hopper proceeded along a passageway that narrowed until they had to crawl on their bellies. The tight confines didn't stop them. A dead end did. The only Medusa xenoforms they found were paintings on a wall.

"Team Dragonfly reporting negative contact. Heading back to chamber 15," the commander told the other teams via her helmet comm.

"Roger that," came the replies.

"Well, no action here," Commander Dragonfly muttered as she turned around to crawl back down the cramped tunnel. Hopper followed her.

Suddenly, the comm system erupted with shouts. The sound of commotion echoed through the tunnels.

"Report! Report!" the commander shouted as she and Hopper squirmed through the dark tunnel. She watched the pings on her wrist computer.

"Team Burrow reporting! Xenoform sighted! We're in pursuit!" Lt Locust replied breathlessly.

CHAPTER 3

"All teams converge on Burrow's position!" Dragonfly ordered.

The rest of Bug Team Alpha hurried through the tunnels. They arrived at a chamber that was on the map schematic but had not yet been explored by the archaeologists.

There were no lamps, no tools and no footprints except those of a xenoform leading into the dark. Burrow and Locust waited for their teammates. They aimed their weapons into the shadows.

"We've got it cornered," Locust reported.

"Wedge formation. High caution," Commander Dragonfly instructed.

The Bug Team flared out behind their commander. Their scope lights swept the black expanse. The beams illuminated painted walls and more hard clay cylinders.

But no xenoform.

"No vibes," Lt Radar said.

"Where'd it go?" Lt Burrow growled. Burrow swung his scope light all over the walls and ceiling. Paintings of the Medusa xenoforms were everywhere. Suddenly, one of the images moved.

Bug Team Alpha shot at the moving image with their blasters on stun power. When they stopped, there was no sign of the xenoform, but there was a new opening where the creature had broken through the wall.

"Radar, I need a scan of whatever's beyond that opening. What can you pick up from the other side?" Commander Dragonfly asked.

"Vibes. Large chamber. Single individual," the lieutenant replied.

"Let's take a look and see what's in there," Dragonfly said and tossed a flare through the newly formed hole and into the dark.

The Medusa xenoform stood in the centre of a large, empty room. It shielded its reptilian eyes from the bright light of the flare. It made no move to attack. Bug Team Alpha surrounded the creature. It lifted up all of its snakelike tendrils as if in surrender.

The Medusa's movements triggered something. The Bug Team heard a grinding sound, and then the floor suddenly dropped out from under their feet. A pair of thick metal slabs fell open like a gigantic trap door. The Bug Team slid down them towards a lower chamber.

"Look out!" Impact shouted.

"Whoa!" Burrow exclaimed as he tried to plunge his arm spikes into the metal to stop his fall. It didn't work. He slid into the hole.

"Evasive action!" Dragonfly ordered.

Commander Dragonfly and Lt Locust deployed their wings and buzzed into the air. Lt Hopper grabbed Lt Radar and tried to jump from slab to slab to keep from falling. He failed. They tumbled into the pit with Impact and Burrow. The flare fell with them and then went out. The darkness was absolute.

"Bug Team, report!" Commander Dragonfly ordered over the comm.

"We're not alone in here," Radar whispered cautiously into her comm.

Commander Dragonfly and Lt Locust hovered above the trapdoor and tossed more flares down into the chamber. The flares immediately illuminated a multitude of tall Medusa figures surrounding the Bug Team on the lower level of the chamber. The team suddenly found themselves confronted by a horde of Medusa hostiles.

"What are th– … Look out!" Impact blurted. Then she rushed towards the Medusas with her blaster blazing. Her hard exoskeleton burst the xenoforms into shards of pottery. Her weapon did the rest.

"Cease fire! They're statues!" Commander Dragonfly said.

Lt Impact followed orders but did not relax. There was no sign of the Medusa that led them there.

"Well, that was unexpected," Hopper observed as he tried to bring his heart rate back to normal. "What is this place?"

"This chamber isn't on the dig map," Dragonfly said as she and Locust descended into the chamber. "We're off the charts."

"There's that stink again!" Lt Hopper gagged.

"And there's the reason. Mummies," Lt Burrow said as he pointed his light at a pile of cocoons that had fallen out of the shattered clay statues. Dozens more lay in a radius around them.

"Those aren't statues. They're coffins. We're in a Medusa burial tomb," Commander Dragonfly realized. She panned her scope light around the chamber. "There are hundreds of them in here."

A thick, smelly ooze was draining out of the broken interiors and spreading across the floor. It moved quickly towards the Bug Team.

"Yuck. Is that embalming liquid?" Lt Radar gasped and held her nose.

"Ow! It burns!" Lt Hopper yelped as some of the goo touched his footpads. He jumped into the air and landed on top of one of the intact statues.

The moment he alighted on the clay figure it burst open. He leaped to another statue. It shattered too. The shards hit other statues and caused them to rupture. It started a chain reaction.

"Evacuate!" the commander ordered. Bug Team Alpha mobilized immediately.

Lt Locust grabbed Lt Radar and flew her out of the chamber. Lt Burrow used the strength of his digging limbs to give Hopper an extra boost to jump up and out of the tomb. Impact and Burrow had no easy escape. They were trapped.

The coffin statues continued to burst and drain caustic liquid into the burial chamber. An acidic flood flowed towards the two stranded Bug Team members.

Commander Dragonfly could have easily flown out of the chamber to safety, but she stood beside Burrow and Impact and faced the danger with them.

"I can buy us some time," Burrow said as he plunged his arm spikes into the dirt floor and swiftly dug a narrow trench two metres deep and five metres long between them and the flowing goo.

"Locust! Buzz down here and help me lift Impact. Radar! Hopper! Secure and drop a line to Burrow," Commander Dragonfly said.

As Locust and Dragonfly lifted Impact out of the tomb, Radar and Hopper threw a rope down to Burrow. He climbed up the lifeline just as the acidic liquid overflowed the trench. The team regrouped at the edge of the tomb opening.

"The xenoform could be anywhere in the dig by now," Commander Dragonfly said. "Until we can capture it, none of the archaeologists are safe. I'm going to order an evacuation. Let's get back to the camp."

✳ ✳ ✳

When Bug Team Alpha emerged from the pyramid mound, they found the camp in an uproar. People were shouting. Supply crates and field equipment were knocked over. Archaeological specimens were scattered from one end of the camp to the other.

"What happened here?" Commander Dragonfly wanted to know.

"You're back!" Dr Leialoha said as she ran up to the team. "A second xenoform attacked the camp while you were away."

"Maybe it's the same one we encountered in the pyramid," Commander Dragonfly wondered.

"Well, at least we know where it went," Burrow muttered.

"It wrecked the place until it found the other xenoform," Dr Leialoha said. "Then it carried its counterpart away into the woods."

"So now there are two of them that we know of on the loose. There could be more," the commander stated. "That's it. Those things are definitely a clear and present danger. Everybody pack up. This camp is being evacuated now."

"What? Wait! No! We can't just pack up and leave! What about all our work? It's taken us two years to collect the data we have, and we've only just scratched the surface!" Dr Leialoha protested.

The commander gave her a look that said this was not up for discussion.

"What I mean is, night is coming and the camp isn't secure," Leialoha said. "It might not be safe for my team to be outside packing up specimens and equipment. And we don't want to lose all our hard work in the process."

"Locust. Hopper. Go get the protective zap fencing from the *Arion* and start setting it up around the camp. We're spending the night here," Commander Dragonfly ordered.

CHAPTER 4

Locust and Hopper set up the perimetre fencing as the Sun dropped below the planet's horizon. It was almost fully dark when they finished placing the energy pillars in the ground.

The two Bug Team members set up the portable energy packs and turned on the power. Suddenly, horizontal bands of brilliant light circled the camp, including the entrance to the dig. Commander Dragonfly tossed a fist-sized rock into the bands to test its capabilities.

Zaaap! The rock shattered into pieces.

"Zap fence is operational. Camp is secure. Get packing, everyone!" Commander Dragonfly declared. "Go! Go! Go! This is an evacuation."

The archaeologists began to shut down their research project. Even though everyone was scared, no one was happy about abandoning the work. As the Bug Team helped with the packing, Dr Leialoha approached Commander Dragonfly.

"I need to talk to you, Commander. In private," Dr Leialoha said. "I've made a, um . . . disturbing observation."

Dragonfly and Leialoha found a secluded spot between two buildings where the Hover Hogs were parked.

"I didn't say anything before, but I got a good look at the second xenoform that attacked the camp," Leialoha started. "I'm certain there was a wedding ring on one of its tendrils."

"A wedding ring?" the commander repeated. "And the first missing person is married to the second one who's now gone missing. Is that correct?"

"Yes. Both Franks have disappeared," Dr Leialoha confirmed.

"Do you think that the Medusa took the ring as a trophy?" Commander Dragonfly wondered.

"I don't know what to think," Leialoha admitted. "It strikes me as very odd. But maybe . . ."

Suddenly, an urgent shout erupted over Dragonfly's comm, interrupting Dr Leialoha's thought.

"Incoming!"

"Report!" Commander Dragonfly demanded. "Give me specifics."

Before any member of the Bug Team Alpha could respond to their commander's orders, something massive smashed through the zap fence. The power packs sparked and flared like fireworks in the dark as the Bug Team raced to converge on the break in the defensive perimeter.

"Bug Team Alpha! Go! Go! Go!" Commander Dragonfly shouted at the top of her voice. The team did not need their comm units to hear her.

Dragonfly deployed her wings and lifted into the air. Below she saw a herd of the native grazing animals ploughing through the energy barrier and stampeding into the camp. They were as big as buffalo and looked like them too, except they had six legs. They used their large curved horns to batter their way through the camp.

"Locust! Get airborne! Diversionary buzz! Impact! Burrow! Defensive line! Radar, Hopper, blasters on heavy stun only. Fire at will," Dragonfly ordered her team over her helmet comm.

Commander Dragonfly knew this was a recovering life form and respected it. She did not want her team to kill any of them. She knew this would be Dr Leialoha's directive as well, especially about the Medusas.

As archaeologists fled into the protective polycrete buildings, Bug Team Alpha took a stand against the threat. Hopper and Radar fired their weapons towards

the oncoming mass. They used their blasters to stun and startle the animals.

Impact and Burrow used their powerful bodies to slam into a few of the beasts, deflecting them in the other direction. Dragonfly and Locust swooped over the herd like hawks, helping to drive them out of the camp.

The herd lumbered into the nearby forest and down the path towards the landing site.

"Um, they're heading for the *Arion*," Locust noticed.

"Locust, grab Hopper and go check on the ship," Commander Dragonfly said.

The lieutenant obeyed exactly as ordered. He swooped down and plucked his comrade from the ground in one smooth motion and flew off in the direction of the landing site.

As the rest of the team reset the zap fence, the archaeologists slowly came out of the buildings. Commander Dragonfly overheard them talking about the animals.

"Why would they stampede like that?"

"They always avoid the camp."

"They're afraid of humans."

"What could have spooked them?"

The commander started to think that the stampede had been deliberate. She wondered if one or both of the Medusa xenoforms had started it. But why? What was the purpose? Simple destruction? Or was it a diversion? What if the xenoforms had used the herd to break down the zap fence to gain access to the pyramid? The fence surrounded the whole camp, including the entrance to the pyramid mound. If the Medusas wanted to get back into the dig, they had to get past the energy fence.

"What if they used the herd like a battering ram, and then used the confusion to divert everyone's attention so they could sneak back into the dig?" Dragonfly speculated to herself out loud. "What is in there that is so important?"

The commander spotted Dr Leialoha and waved her over.

"Doctor, tell me everything you know about that underground pyramid," Dragonfly said.

"Well, we've dated it to be about 10,000 years old," Dr Leialoha began. "From the specimens and evidence we've collected, our theory is that it was built after the meteor swarm wrecked the environment. The Medusa culture was dying off as their food sources diminished.

The events are painted on the walls of certain chambers like a history book. We think the pyramid is a memorial to their civilization. There's no evidence that anyone ever lived there. It wasn't occupied for long periods of time."

"Well, at least not by the living," Commander Dragonfly added.

"No. The only artefacts we've found are the wall paintings and the hundreds of fired clay cylinders," Dr Leialoha replied.

"You can add mummies to that list," the commander said. "The Bug Team encountered a tomb with clay statues that had mummies inside them."

"What?! Where? This is amazing!" Dr Leialoha exclaimed.

"We were in pursuit of the xenoform when it led us into a chamber beyond the mapped sections of the dig. The floor opened up and we fell into the tomb," Commander Dragonfly said. She brought up the dig schematics on her wrist computer. "The nearest recorded coordinates we were given were for chamber 27. It seems to me that you're going to have to update your maps of the dig after this."

"Wait. Did you just say the xenoform led you?" Dr Leialoha asked.

"It looked that way to me," the commander concluded. "I don't know if it was supposed to be a death trap or not, but the corrosive embalming fluid sure made things hazardous."

"Embalming fluid?!" Leialoha gasped. "First you tell me there is an undiscovered tomb full of Medusa mummies in clay coffins. Now you say there was embalming fluid preserving them? What an incredible discovery! I have to see this! I have to go down there!"

"Absolutely not! We're in the middle of an emergency evacuation. Two people are missing, and at least two dangerous creatures are on the loose," Commander Dragonfly reminded her. "I will not allow anyone back into the dig. Not even you, Doctor. It's for your own safety."

Dr Leialoha gave the officer a look that said this was not up for discussion.

"Your mission is to find our two missing archaeologists – and I'm not leaving this planet until you do," she told Dragonfly.

Commander Dragonfly rolled her eyes and got on the comm.

"Dragonfly to Locust. Report your status," the commander said.

"Hopper and I are on the *Arion*," came the reply from Lt Locust. "The herd knocked the ship around. We're checking for hull damage and doing a full systems check to make sure everything is intact and operational. Completion in 30."

"Stay with the ship until further notice and keep me informed of your progress," Dragonfly ordered. "We have to evacuate everyone as soon as possible, and a ship disabled by a lumbering herd of animals is not an acceptable mission component."

Commander Dragonfly deployed her wings and flew towards the rest of her team. Leialoha sprinted to keep pace with the Bug Team leader.

"We're going back into the dig," Dragonfly told her team.

CHAPTER 5

Locust and Hopper stayed with the ship. The rest of Bug Team Alpha reentered the pyramid. There, they spotted a fresh trail of xenoform footprints leading deep into the mound.

The footprints confirmed Dragonfly's earlier suspicion. The Medusas had intentionally spooked the herd, causing the stampede. This created a diversion so the Medusas could get back inside the dig. But she still wondered why. What was so important in there that would force them to take that sort of action?

"They must have reentered the dig during the stampede," Dragonfly noted.

Dr Leialoha followed the team. She was equipped with a high-intensity headlamp and a video recorder. She was excited as they passed beyond the excavated sections of the dig and arrived at chamber 27.

"This is as far as we got. We thought it was a dead end," Dr Leialoha said as she paused inside the room. Then she saw the hole in the far wall. "I notice you found an exit."

"More than that," Commander Dragonfly mentioned.

The team progressed beyond the wall and into the chamber where the floor had fallen out from under them.

"Welcome to chamber 28," Dragonfly said.

Dr Leialoha panned the recorder around the empty room. Her high-intensity headlamp swept across the painted walls.

"These images are different from anything else in the pyramid!" she exclaimed as she rushed to examine them closer.

"Dr Leialoha, I think you might be missing the massive gorilla in the room," Commander Dragonfly said bluntly, pointing to the huge opening in the floor.

Leialoha peered into the opening and gasped as her light illuminated the area below.

"We've explored this dig for two years and have

never come across anything like this," Leialoha said. "Not that I approve of your completely non-scientific methods."

"Commander Dragonfly! Over here! You've got to see this!" Burrow shouted at her from across the chamber. His bright scope light illuminated a large opening in the wall.

"It's a doorway!" Leialoha exclaimed as she directed her headlamp and video recorder along the perimeter.

"That wasn't there before," Impact noted.

"Two new discoveries in the space of a day? I should've had Bug Team Alpha on my archaeology project from the start," Leialoha remarked.

"That's very . . . ," Dragonfly began.

"Footprints!" Radar shouted, cutting off her commander. Her scope spotlighted xenoform marks in the dirt. Her cranial antennae twitched.

The entire team converged on the door opening but did not enter.

"Wedge formation, high caution," Commander Dragonfly ordered the squad. "Doctor, stay here until I give the all clear."

The Bug Team stepped through the dark doorway. The archaeologist, blatantly disobeying the orders, followed them.

"I'm not staying anywhere," Dr Leialoha muttered.

Dr Leialoha forged ahead, but she did not get very far. She quickly found herself jammed up against the Bug Team members in a narrow tunnel. Then one of Burrow's bug arms accidentally poked her in the shoulder.

"Ow!" Dr Leialoha complained loudly. Echoes bounced away into the dark.

"Quiet!" the commander told her sharply. "Radar needs to listen."

The whole team paused. They allowed Lt Radar to sense the vibrations coming towards them in the darkness.

Dr Leialoha tipped her head back, stretching her neck, allowing her headlamp to illuminate carvings on the ceiling she'd never seen before.

"Carvings?!" Dr Leialoha blurted in surprise. The sound of her voice bounced against the walls of the passageway.

"Doctor!" Commander Dragonfly admonished in a low hiss.

The archaeologist frowned in frustration but kept silent.

"The passageway descends in a spiral, about 10 to 20 metres down," Radar reported at last. "Actually, the doctor was rather helpful. Her voice has quite a pitch."

"Did she just call me shrill?" Dr Leialoha muttered as the team moved forwards. No one from the Bug Team responded to her question. They were focused on their mission.

Commander Dragonfly continued to follow the xenoform footprints that led her and the squad down the spiral into the dark. Even with the addition of Dr Leialoha's headlamp, their sight line extended only a few metres.

The spiral curve continually hid what was ahead of them. The corridor was so narrow that the Bug Team had to walk single file.

"New vibe ahead," Lt Radar warned. "It's static. No movement."

The team prepared for a possible ambush. They moved forwards slowly, one pace at a time. But there was no surprise attack.

The Bug Team walked through a section of the corridor that had two metal doors on opposite sides of the passageway. These were what the lieutenant had sensed. The xenoform footprints continued beyond the doors.

"Any vibrations?" Dragonfly asked Radar.

"The doors are too thick for me to read through, but they look like they've been sealed for centuries," Lt Radar said as she scanned her scope light over the surface.

"Then there's no immediate danger to the team or the mission. We keep following the footprints," the commander decided.

As Dragonfly and the Bug Team continued on the trail, Dr Leialoha lingered by the doors. Her curiosity was overwhelming. She reached out to touch the ancient material.

"Doctor!" Commander Dragonfly's voice echoed.

"Huh! Who's shrill now?" Leialoha grumbled.

The archaeologist caught back up with the Bug Team members as they walked down the curving spiral corridor.

Moments later the group encountered two more sets of doors. They appeared undisturbed as well. Dr Leialoha bit her lip and did not comment on the opportunity to stop and closely study the artefacts. What was beyond those doors? Her professional imagination ran wild.

The Medusa xenoform footprints led the team all the way to the bottom of the spiral passageway. The corridor got wider at the very end. It terminated at a gigantic door larger than all the others they'd seen. It was open.

"This is very important," Dr Leialoha said. "We've found the spiral to be an important symbol all over the galaxy, including to the inhabitants of this planet before the devastation. And a spiral has led us here."

"This door has recently been opened," Impact said as she pointed her scope light at the fresh scuffmarks in the dust.

"The prints lead inside," Burrow observed.

Bug Team Alpha readied their weapons and stepped through the massive door. Commander Dragonfly led the way. Her attention was on the footprints illuminated by her scope light. The rest of the chamber was pitch black around her and the squad. Even Dr Leialoha's high-intensity headlamp failed to pierce the darkness.

"Radar?" the commander said.

"We're inside something very, very big," the lieutenant replied. "And we're not alone."

CHAPTER 6

Lt Radar's cranial antennae twitched and vibrated. She tried to sense what was beyond the team in the blackness. She knew the lives and safety of Bug Team Alpha – as well as that of Dr Leialoha and the rest of the archaeologists – depended on it.

"Okay, I've got it now," the lieutenant said. "We're in a chamber 30 metres high and 40 metres wide. The walls slope at an acute angle. Wait a minute. We're in a pyramid!"

"A pyramid within a pyramid? That's amazing! It makes total sense!" Dr Leialoha exclaimed. Her voice echoed against the unseen walls.

"Doctor! Quiet!" Commander Dragonfly hissed. She turned her head towards the archaeologist but kept her weapon aimed forwards.

Dr Leialoha wanted to explain the significance of this discovery. Theories raced through her head.

She began to recall all the things she and her team had learned about the significance of pyramids to the ancient culture. Ideas came to her, but she hugged her arms around her chest and tried to contain her excitement.

"Radar, you said we are not alone. Please specify," Dragonfly said.

"I recognize the vibes now. Two Medusa xenoforms. They are about 20 metres ahead," Lt Radar reported. "No motion. They've stopped in the middle of the chamber in front of something . . . extremely tall and made of stone. I think it's a statue."

"Anything else in a 360 sweep?" Dragonfly asked.

Lt Radar turned in a slow circle and stretched her bug-enhanced senses through the darkness.

"Nothing detected," Radar replied.

"Advance. But hold fire," Commander Dragonfly ordered. "Don't hurt the xenoforms unless it is in self-defence or otherwise ordered to. We need them to lead to us to the Franks."

As the team moved forward, their lights gradually illuminated the shapes of the two Medusa xenoforms.

They were kneeling in front of what looked to be a pair of giant feet.

Dr Leialoha panned her headlamp upwards. The feet were part of an enormous statue of a Medusa. It dominated the centre of the underground pyramid chamber and reached almost to the top. She grew more and more excited.

"This is either their supreme deity or very important royalty," Leialoha whispered in awe.

The doctor took video of the enormous statue. Bright gemstones sparkled like a crown on its head. The end of each tendril had a round opening. She wondered if the tendrils were hollow.

"Are they worshipping it?" Impact wondered. "It almost looks like they're praying."

One of the xenoforms turned at the sound of Impact's voice. It blinked against the bright light of Leialoha's headlamp and raised several tendrils to shield its reptilian eyes.

"It responded!" Dr Leialoha smiled.

Leialoha turned towards Dragonfly, hopeful. "Commander! We might be able to communicate with them!"

But the xenoforms didn't seem interested in talking. They reached out and touched a set of symbols that looked like hieroglyphics carved into the base of the statue. Above, the statue's stone tendrils made a hissing noise. Then it expelled a mist from the openings.

"I don't like the look of this," the commander muttered.

"Or the sound of it," Radar added.

Suddenly, the two xenoforms started to sing in a high pitch. It was not a pleasant sound to human ears. Lt Radar grabbed her forehead in pain. The sound was too much for her sensitive antennae to bear. Dr Leialoha clapped her hands to her ears and almost dropped her video recorder.

"Let's get out of here!" Commander Dragonfly ordered.

It was too late. Hundreds of objects the size and shape of sea urchins flew out from the openings in the statue's tendrils. These spiny creatures gathered high in the shadows of the pyramid. Then they sped straight towards the Bug Team members and Dr Leialoha.

"Shoot those things down! Fire at will!" Dragonfly commanded.

The Bug Team's fire was futile. It was like shooting at a swarm of bees. A large percentage of the fist-sized spiny globes broke though the team's first line of defence.

Impact's hard exoskeleton protected her from the worst of the attack. The objects bounced off her tough carapace.

Commander Dragonfly revved her wings to a speed that created a barrier of air pressure between her and the threat.

Burrow used his bug arms to swipe the oncoming spheres away.

All Dr Leialoha could do was bat at the swarm with her hands.

"Hey, look! These are mechanical! They're drones!" Burrow shouted in surprise as he plucked one of the "sea urchins" off his arm.

"Nice to know!" Lt Radar said sarcastically as she tried to fend off an attack. Her combat armour was the only protection between her and the enemy's sharp barbs.

Dr Leialoha did not have that protection.

"Owww!" Leialoha howled as a drone struck her on an exposed wrist. She dropped her video recorder to grasp her wounded limb.

"Bug Team, fall back!" Commander Dragonfly shouted.

The team surrounded Leialoha in a protective circle. They headed for the exit as they continued to shoot at the swarm.

Leialoha stumbled along with the team, but she kept her attention on the small, oval object quickly moving under the upper layers of her skin where she had been struck by a drone. It was shaped like a scarab beetle and crawled swiftly from her wrist to her shoulder.

"That drone thing implanted something in me as it hit my wrist," Leialoha said. "I can feel it working its way up my arm."

The tiny implant climbed over her shoulder blade and then clamped onto her spine at the base of her skull.

"It looks a like a –" Dr Leialoha tried to say before fainting.

"I've got you, Doctor," Impact said as she caught the collapsing archaeologist. Then the lieutenant immediately saw something that shocked even her.

"She's . . . she's . . . changing!" Impact gasped in surprise.

Dr Leialoha's body started to shape-shift. Every bit of her skin began to form scales. Her shirt shredded as snakelike tendrils budded out of her torso and quickly grew.

"She's turning into one of them! Dr Leialoha is becoming a Medusa!" Impact realized.

Impact slung Leialoha over her shoulder as Bug Team Alpha fought their way out of the lower chamber and back up the spiral ramp.

The drone swarm followed the group every step of the way. Blaster fire knocked out dozens of drones at a time, but that did not seem to make an impact on the assault.

"How's the doctor doing?" Commander Dragonfly asked between weapons fire.

"She's still out of it," Lt Impact replied as she held the unconscious archaeologist over her shoulder with one hand and shot at the drones with the other. "But she's still transforming."

"We've got to get her to the medical doctor on the surface. Fast!" Dragonfly said. "Bug Team Alpha. Go! Go! Go!"

The elite team surged up the spiral ramp.

CHAPTER 7

The drones pursued Bug Team Alpha up the slope of the spiral corridor like a swarm of angry insects. The team had learned that just one clear hit by the enemy drones would result in a Medusa transformation. Dr Leialoha was living proof.

Although it had been difficult to travel the narrow passageway on the way down, it benefited them on the way up.

"Narrow-focus firepower!" Commander Dragonfly instructed as the drones followed the group.

The Bug Team concentrated their weapon fire within the tight confines of the tunnel. They blasted the formation of enemy drones. There was nowhere else for the swarm to spread. In the end nothing was left but black dust.

"Yes!" Burrow cheered and flared his arm spikes.

"Keep moving," Commander Dragonfly said sharply before her team started to celebrate too much and lose concentration.

The team jogged up the spiral pathway. Impact carried Dr Leialoha as the unconscious archaeologist continued to transform. They made it to the upper chambers and ran out through the newly discovered chamber 28. That's when a second wave of drones swarmed up out of the spiral corridor and buzzed around the Bug Team.

A portion of the drone swarm flew down through the opening to the mummy chamber. They landed on the cocoons and stabbed their barbs into the burial shrouds.

Whatever had crawled under Dr Leialoha's skin now did the same thing to the mummy wrappings. Moments later the shrouds split open. The mummies rose to their feet. A door opened automatically. Hundreds of reanimated Medusas started to shamble from the tomb.

Bug Team Alpha ran out of the dig and into the night-time camp. The drone swarm emerged right behind them.

"Everybody! Get to safety, now!" Commander Dragonfly shouted at the archaeologists who were still outside packing up their equipment.

The commander launched herself into the air and fired at the massed threat behind her team. The blaster barrage motivated the scientists. They dropped what they were doing and ran into various polycrete buildings for safety.

The drones scattered in pursuit of the fleeing humans. Bug Team Alpha took a stand in the centre of the camp. Team members shot at the drones with their blasters as they spread out.

The Bug Team's defence wasn't enough to prevent some of the archaeologists from being hit. They fell to the ground and started to transform into Medusas.

And then the reanimated Medusa mummies poured out of the pyramid.

"What now – Medusa *zombies*?" Radar yelled when she saw the withered corpses running towards the team. "This op is officially weird!"

"Bug Team! Fall back to the Infirmary!" Dragonfly ordered as the creatures rushed the camp.

Lt Impact led the way. Dr Leialoha was still slumped over her shoulder. Radar and Burrow followed. Dragonfly provided cover fire from above.

The Bug Team members reached the Infirmary. They slammed the door shut and barricaded themselves against it. Impact placed Leialoha on the exam table.

"What are those things?" Dr Barrington asked breathlessly as he hurried to lock down a steel window shutter. Medusa zombies pounded their shrivelled tentacles against the metal. Drone impacts sounded like scattershot.

Then Dr Barrington saw the Medusa on the table. He had to look twice to realize that something was drastically different about this one. Not only was the xenoform half human, he recognized the human half.

"Dr Leialoha!" he gasped. "What happened?"

"She got hit by one of those drone things and started to turn into a Medusa," Commander Dragonfly reported.

"I can feel my cells changing," Leialoha whispered. "There are waves of alien thoughts flooding my mind. Medusa memories!"

Dr Barrington activated the exam table's diagnostic scanner. A holographic image appeared directly above the patient. The image was a mash-up of human and Medusa physiology. It confirmed that what was happening to the outside of Dr Leialoha's body was happening on the inside as well. Everyone watched organs and bones mutate before their eyes.

"Is there anything you can do to stop the process?" Dragonfly asked.

"I don't know," Dr Barrington admitted as he studied the holographic image intently.

Suddenly, he pointed at a shadow on the scan.

"There's a foreign object at the base of her skull. It's nothing I recognize," he stated.

"We've got to assume it's Medusan," Commander Dragonfly concluded. "Remove it."

"I have no way of knowing what effect that might have. There could be long-lasting damage. The procedure could even kill her," the physician said as he hesitated.

"Or it could save her life," Dragonfly said. "Do it."

"No! I'm . . . *learning* about them," Dr Leialoha protested weakly.

Dr Barrington, following Commander Dragonfly's orders, activated a sedation field and deployed a laser scalpel that sliced through the layers of reptilian scales. Then he used a surgical extractor to remove the object.

Immediately, the transformation stopped.

"Looks like you saved her," Lt Impact observed.

Dr Barrington sealed up the incision. Then he examined the object under a magnifying scanner. A holographic image was displayed. The device had long, thin tendrils coming out of a central disk.

"It looks like a spider," Lt Radar said. "Yuck. I hate spiders."

Burrow tickled Radar on the back of the neck like a spider's legs and made her jump.

"You know what? Seeing Dr Leialoha like this makes me think the same thing happened to the Franks," Dr Barrington realized. "They must have come across something in the dig that turned them into Medusa xenoforms. First Laurel and then Millerd."

"I think you're right," Commander Dragonfly agreed. "Leialoha told me she saw one of the Medusas wearing a wedding ring on its tendril. I thought the xenoform had taken it as a trophy. But if it was actually one of the Franks . . ."

"Our colleagues aren't missing. They're transformed," Barrington concluded.

He turned to look at the Medusan implant device still in the scanner.

"Hmmm. If I can reverse-engineer this thing I might be able to reverse Dr Leialoha's transformation – and the Franks'."

"Get on that, Doctor. I think there are a number of your colleagues who are going to need it," Dragonfly said. "I saw a lot of them get hit by the drones outside."

"I'll do my best," Dr Barrington assured her.

A moment later Dragonfly faced a new challenge.

"*Arion* to Commander Dragonfly! Come in!" Lt Locust's urgent voice came over the comm.

"Go ahead, *Arion*," the commander responded.

"Those big beasts are back and ramming the ship," Lt Locust reported. "They're really serious about it this time. And they look . . . *weird*."

"Specify," Dragonfly declared.

"They've got those snakelike tendrils all over their bodies," Locust replied.

Suddenly, Commander Dragonfly heard a new sound transmitted over the comm. It was like hail hitting the hull.

"Commander, the *Arion* is under attack by swarms of . . . giant bees with spikes?" Lt Locust shouted.

"They're Medusa drones, and they're dangerous," Commander Dragonfly said. "Lift off and get to a secure location. Do not come to the base until I say so. That's an order."

"Understood. Initiating lift off," Locust replied.

The commander listened to the normal chatter of flight procedures until a scramble of shouts from Locust and Hopper came over the comm.

"They're following!"

"Fire at will!"

"No good! No good!"

"They're trying to get through the hull!"

"Head for orbit!"

"Suck vacuum!"

The communications link burst into static and Commander Dragonfly lost contact with the *Arion*.

CHAPTER 8

"Commander! Something's happening!" Lt Radar said. "Well, actually something's not happening. I don't hear anything from outside anymore. No more vibes at all."

Commander Dragonfly and the others listened carefully to the sound of silence outside. The reanimated Medusa zombies had stopped battering themselves against the buildings. The drones had stopped buzzing around the camp.

"Recon," Commander Dragonfly said.

The commander braced herself to open the Infirmary door. Impact and Burrow flanked her with weapons ready.

"I'm opening the door in one . . . two . . . ," Dragonfly counted as she deactivated an electronic lock.

The commander inhaled a deep breath to prepare herself for immediate action. Then slowly she opened the door. The bright sunlight of a new day streamed into the Infirmary. Commander Dragonfly stepped outside with her weapon raised.

Bug Team Alpha followed their leader. They saw a wrecked camp. Equipment, vehicles and every specimen case was turned on its side and scattered. Even the Bug Team's Hover Hogs were knocked over. Commander Dragonfly looked at the damage. But there was something missing.

"No bodies," she observed. "There are no dead. No wounded. Everyone who was outside must have been hit by the drones and transformed into Medusas. But how many? Bug Team Alpha, search the camp for survivors of the attack. I want a head count as soon as possible," Dragonfly ordered.

As Burrow, Radar and Impact fanned out to begin the search, Commander Dragonfly suddenly heard a blaster shot. Something exploded close to her head, but she didn't flinch. A drone fell to the ground.

"Sorry, commander," Lt Impact yelled from a few metres out. "No time for a heads-up."

"Watch out for strays," Dragonfly warned the rest of her team over her helmet comm.

"Commander . . . Dragon . . . fly," a voice said from behind the commander.

Dragonfly turned to see the semi-transformed Dr Leialoha leaning against the door of the Infirmary building. She had managed to climb off the exam table and take a few steps. The archaeologist was still half human and half Medusa. She shielded her eyes against the bright sunlight with one human arm and a few Medusa tentacles.

Upon seeing this, the commander had a sudden realization.

"The Medusa xenoforms can't tolerate the sunlight. They're *nocturnal*," Dragonfly announced as she guided Leialoha back into the Infirmary. "We've seen them only inside the dig or at night. The only time one of them came into the daylight was to rescue one of its own from the Infirmary. Even the drones and the zombies retreated at dawn. This information is an important tactical advantage."

"I can feel them," Leialoha said quietly. "The Medusas are about to rise."

"What, more zombies?" Dragonfly asked sharply. "How many? Where?"

"We . . . they . . . my transformed colleagues . . . are gathering in the pyramid," Leialoha said. She shook her head as if to clear it. "Sorry. I seem to have two minds. I'm both human and Medusa right now."

"If they're in the pyramid, we can trap them there. Forever," Dragonfly stated. Then she activated her helmet comm. "Bug Team Alpha, prepare to seal the dig!"

"No!" Leialoha protested. "Those are my friends and co-workers down there. I . . . you can't abandon them."

"Honestly, Dr Leialoha, I don't know how to save them," Commander Dragonfly admitted.

"I think I know how," Dr Barrington interrupted. "I've been studying the Medusa implant. It's designed to inject Medusa DNA into any organic species and rewrite the host DNA. Humans become Medusa. Herding beasts become Medusa."

"What about a human spliced with insect DNA?" Dragonfly asked. "Is Bug Team Alpha in danger?"

"Perhaps, but that's beyond my area of expertise, I'm afraid." Dr Barrington shrugged. "I'm a field physician, not a genetic surgeon."

"Maybe the technology that created Bug Team Alpha can cure my friends," Leialoha appealed to Commander Dragonfly. "Maybe the doctors can figure out how to use the Medusa tech to revert us. Please. Rescue the other archaeologists."

"That's my mission," the commander agreed. "But we've got to get them out of the pyramid first. I need that head count to . . ."

Suddenly, Lt Locust's voice burst over Dragonfly's helmet comm.

"*Arion* to Dragonfly!" Locust said. "Can you hear me?"

"I read you, *Arion*. Glad to hear your voice. What's your status?" the commander responded.

"We achieved a stable orbit. The drones dropped off at negative psi levels. They can't take the vacuum," Locust replied. "All ship's functions are nominal. We're ready to return and commence evacuation of the dig."

"Return to the designated landing site," Dragonfly ordered.

"On our way," Lt Locust confirmed.

"Now, I've just got to go and get the people we were sent here to rescue," Dragonfly muttered to herself.

A moment later, Burrow, Radar and Impact entered the Infirmary to give their report to their commanding officer.

"Commander, we have the head count you requested," Lt Burrow said and showed Dragonfly a list on his wrist computer. "Out of the 24 scientists on this project, 12 are missing and presumed transformed. That includes the two Franks."

"That's half the camp," the commander realized. "They aren't going to be cooperative in their transformed state."

"This might help," Dr Barrington said. He handed Dragonfly a small medical device. "I tweaked a laser scalpel and put it together with a surgical extractor. You can use it to remove the Medusa implants from our colleagues. Hopefully that will restore their minds, like it did for Dr Leialoha."

"Which is why I'm going with you," Leialoha stated. "They'll listen to me."

"I hope you're right, because sealing the pyramid is my only other option," the commander stated bluntly. "Bug Team Alpha – move out!"

Burrow and Impact ran out of the Infirmary. They picked up their knocked-over Hover Hogs and jumped on. Radar followed them and grabbed her Bug Bike.

The team assembled around their commanding officer. Dragonfly raised an eyebrow in response to their independent action.

"We might have a need for some speed," Impact said with a grin.

"Agreed. Let's make this quick," Dragonfly said.

The commander jumped onto the back of Impact's Hover Hog. Burrow pulled Leialoha up behind him on his vehicle.

"Everybody! Listen closely! Our ship is coming for you! Evacuation from this planet is in 30! Take only what you can carry! It's grab and go!" Dragonfly shouted at the archaeologists finally emerging from the buildings after the attack. "Move!"

The Bug Team sped into the pyramid mound. The sound of the Hover Hogs vibrated against the walls of the ancient chambers as the vehicles roared down the passageways. There was no need to follow a trail of footprints now. Dr Leialoha knew where her transformed friends were gathered. She felt the same mental pull of ancient memories that they did.

"Everyone is in the Resurrection Chamber," Dr Leialoha shouted over the roar of the Hogs.

"The *what*?" Commander Dragonfly asked sharply. "What do you mean by resurrection? More zombies?"

"No, more *Medusas* . . . ," Leialoha said.

Commander Dragonfly knew that more Medusas meant more trouble.

CHAPTER 9

Bug Team Alpha rode their vehicles through the upper chambers without encountering any drones or zombies. When they entered the spiral passageway, they were stopped in their tracks. It was jammed full of withered Medusa zombies. The narrow corridor was packed like a clogged drain.

"There's only one way to clear a path. Fire at will," Commander Dragonfly ordered as she lifted her blaster.

The rest of Bug Team Alpha took aim.

"No!" Dr Leialoha protested. "You'll kill them!"

"They're zombies. They're already dead," Dragonfly replied.

"No! They're reanimated. There's a difference," Leialoha insisted. "It's part of the plan."

"What plan?" the commander asked warily. She did not lower her weapon.

"The Medusa memories inside my mind . . . they're telling me . . . there are so many thoughts inside my head. I think . . . the reanimated mummies are protectors," Leialoha struggled to explain. "The drones awakened them for this purpose."

"I've got too many questions about too many things right now and no time for answers," Commander Dragonfly said. "Our top priority is to get to the transformed archaeologists in the lower chamber and get them out of here, and we have to get through that horde to do so. You've got the Medusa mind, Doctor. Any suggestions?"

"I do have an idea," Leialoha said as she climbed down off the Hover Hog.

The semi-transformed scientist walked up to the reanimated mummies and raised her tentacles. The mass shifted around to look at her. Then they suddenly stood back to let her pass. There was just enough room for her to squeeze through.

"Follow me," Leialoha told the Bug Team.

The team dismounted from their vehicles and entered the passageway on foot. Dragonfly folded her wings tightly and pressed past the throng. Lt Radar's slim form slipped through the mass with little trouble. Impact and Burrow jostled their bulky bodies against the milling mummies as they worked their way down the spiral corridor.

"Oof. This is worse than the crowds during the High Fest Days on Gaia 6," Impact muttered.

"Don't remind me," Burrow responded.

The Bug Team shuffled down the spiral path slowly, step by step. Along the way they noticed that the doors that had been sealed for centuries were now open.

Leialoha had wanted to see what was inside when the Bug Team had first come down the spiral corridor. Now she had the chance. She used her tentacles to move the mummies aside. She peered past the doorway and saw hundreds of reanimated Medusas standing inside the tombs. None of them moved. It was as if they were waiting for instructions.

"It looks like another memorial chamber full of clay statue coffins, and all of them have been broken. Thousands of them," Leialoha observed. "Somehow the drones got through the doors – or the doors opened automatically – and then they reanimated the mummies."

Commander Dragonfly did not respond, but she took in the information as Dr Leialoha continued to lead the team down to the bottom of the spiral path. When they entered the pyramid chamber, the reanimated mummies remained outside. Inside the chamber the air was thick with an extremely strong smell. The source became obvious the moment the team stepped inside the room.

"Eggs?" Commander Dragonfly gagged as she held her nose. "Where did they come from?"

The floor was covered with huge slimy pods. In the middle of the room, at the base of the Medusa statue, stood the transformed archaeologists. Their bodies swayed as if in a trance. They waved their tentacles in the air as something large moved under their scales. Eggs emerged from the ends of the tendrils and plopped onto the floor. As the eggs rolled a short distance across the floor, they grew from the size of a goose egg to the size of a watermelon.

"What is going on?" Dragonfly asked.

"We are in the Resurrection Chamber," Dr Leialoha replied, her voice full of awe. "It's the birth of a new generation. The Medusa race is being reborn."

"You mean they're having babies?" Impact gasped. "Eww."

"This is what you were talking about earlier, isn't it?" Dragonfly said to Dr Leialoha.

The commander waded through the piles of egg pods and worked her way towards the transformed scientists. She applied Dr Barrington's extraction device to the neck of the nearest one. The DNA implant popped out. Dragonfly put it into a pouch on her combat belt to take back to Dr Barrington. He was going to need multiple specimens of the Medusan implant tech if he was going to cure his colleagues.

As soon as the DNA implant was removed, the creature's egg production stopped. The Medusa blinked its reptilian eyes and looked around in confusion.

"Where . . . where am I?" the transformed archaeologist asked as the commander repeated the procedure with the rest of the scientists.

"Do you know who you are?" Dr Leialoha asked as she gently put her human hand on its shoulder.

"I'm Joshua Levitz," the Medusa replied. "Leialoha? Is that you? What happened to you?"

"The same thing that happened to you," Leialoha replied. "Well, almost."

The archaeologist looked down at his body. He saw the scales and tentacles and shrieked in surprise. Then he looked around at his surroundings and shrieked some more.

"Easy! Easy! Josh, it's all right!" Dr Leialoha said, trying to calm her colleague. "What's the last thing you remember?"

"I was in camp packing my artefact samples. Then those flying things came out of the dig," Levitz replied. "One of them bit me."

"It wasn't a bite, Josh. A drone injected a device that rewrote your DNA. You turned into a Medusa!" Leialoha explained.

As Commander Dragonfly finished extracting the Medusa implants from the rest of the scientists, their minds and identities came back to them. Their bodies did not. There were shouts of surprise and shock. Two rose above the rest.

"Laurel!"

"Millerd!"

The two Franks embraced when they recognized each other despite their xenoform bodies.

"The reunion will have to wait," Commander Dragonfly said gently. "We've got to get out of here. The zombies are getting restless."

The mass of reanimated mummies in the corridor shifted nervously as if they sensed something was wrong.

"We stopped the resurrection cycle," Leialoha said. "They're the protectors, remember? That probably makes us the enemy right now."

"Well, that's nothing new. We've been on the defensive this whole mission," the commander pointed out. "Dr Leialoha. Do you think you can lead us through the mass again? Otherwise we'll be forced to shoot our way out."

"Yes, of course," Dr Leialoha responded. "But . . . are you sure we can't stay for a little while to study the chamber and the eggs? We don't know anything about either of them. Maybe I could just . . ."

Bug Team Alpha snapped into formation behind their commanding officer to reinforce her statement.

"Okay! Never mind!" Dr Leialoha said and lifted her tentacles in surrender.

Dr Leialoha began leading the transformed archaeologists out of the Resurrection Chamber. The reanimated Medusa mummies stepped back to allow them to pass.

Dragonfly and the Bug Team followed. The entire throng of zombies suddenly turned to face the opening of the Resurrection Chamber. Lt Radar's antennae twitched wildly.

"Commander!" Radar shouted. "I'm getting massive vibes from back inside the chamber! It's the eggs. Something's happening!"

CHAPTER 10

Commander Dragonfly turned on one heel and aimed her weapon back into the Resurrection Chamber, ready for any threat that faced her. That's when she saw the egg pods splitting open. Larval life forms crawled out and flapped tiny tentacles. The stench was incredible.

"They're hatching!" Dragonfly warned.

Dr Leialoha shoved her way back into the chamber. She gazed at the writhing mass of newborns.

"It's the resurrection! This was their plan!" Leialoha concluded. "They waited for a compatible life form to arrive to transform into Medusas who could produce a new generation of eggs! We humans were obviously compatible."

"What about the grazing animals? They grew tentacles," Dragonfly asked.

"But they didn't turn completely into Medusas like we did," Leialoha replied. "Their transformation didn't go far enough."

The nearest portion of the wriggling swarm seemed to respond to Leialoha's voice. They scuttled towards her using their infant tendrils like spider legs.

"Hello, little ones," Dr Leialoha said softly and extended a tentacle to them.

CHOMP! The newborns bit her!

"Ow!" Leialoha howled. She looked at her tentacle. Purple ooze seeped out of the wound.

"They're hungry," Leialoha realized as Medusa memories were triggered in her mind. "They're born ravenous! We're in trouble!"

"Bug Team Alpha! Go! Go! Go!" Commander Dragonfly ordered.

Lt Impact took the lead up the spiral corridor. She used her tough exoskeleton to bulldoze through the reanimated mummies crowding the passageway. They toppled into each other and fell to the floor, but Lt Burrow used his arm and leg spikes to toss them out of the way. Lt Radar led the group of transformed archaeologists in the wake of Impact and Burrow. Commander Dragonfly and Dr Leialoha brought up the rear. Thousands of hungry larval Medusa mouths followed them up the spiral path.

Commander Dragonfly pointed her weapon at the ceiling and fired a blast. The roof came down, and the rubble sealed the corridor between them and the ravenous larval Medusas.

"That should hold them," the commander said.

Immediately, the pile of rubble started to shift and fall.

"Or not," Burrow observed.

"Impact, take Leialoha and get to the surface quick," Commander Dragonfly instructed. "Get the camp moving. I want them halfway to the landing site by the time the rest of us get out of here."

"Will do, Commander. Come on, Doc, you're with me," the lieutenant replied as she hoisted the archaeologist over her shoulder and started to run.

As Impact and Leialoha raced ahead, the transformed archaeologists continued up the spiral passageway with Dragonfly, Radar and Burrow protecting them from behind. They squeezed past Medusa mummies that stood unmoving in the corridor. Dragonfly didn't know if they were dormant or simply waiting for instructions. She was just grateful for the lack of resistance.

When the group finally emerged from the dig and into the sunlight, the transformed archaeologists shielded their eyes against the glare. The camp was empty. Impact and Leialoha had succeeded in getting everyone moving.

"Burrow, contact the *Arion* for an ETA. Then you and Radar get these . . . er . . . people to the landing site," Commander Dragonfly ordered as she pulled a pair of grenades from her combat belt.

As the commander attached the explosives to the entrance of the dig, Dr Leialoha ran up to her wearing a baseball cap and a pair of sunglasses that she had grabbed from her room. A sheet covered her body like a poncho to protect her from the Sun. The sight was so odd that Dragonfly paused what she was doing.

"Commander, you can't blow up the dig!" Leialoha protested.

"Give me one good reason why not," Dragonfly replied and resumed her task.

"Because this is *their* planet. Let them out. Let them live in it," Dr Leialoha said. "They've waited thousands of years for this."

"Okay, that's more than one good reason," Commander Dragonfly agreed with a sigh. She shoved the grenades back onto her belt. "Let's get out of here."

Dragonfly grabbed Dr Leialoha by a tentacle and deployed her wings. She flew into the forest just as the larval Medusas poured out of the pyramid. The newborns were dazzled by the sunlight but it did not stop them. Their need for food was stronger than their nocturnal nature. They sensed their prey – Dragonfly and Leialoha – and headed in pursuit of their first meal.

When Commander Dragonfly and Dr Leialoha arrived at the landing site, the rest of the Bug Team and all the archaeologists were there. The ship was not. Without it, there was no escape from the horde of carnivorous larval Medusas heading for them.

"Looks like our ride is late," Burrow told the commander sourly.

"*Arion*! Where are you?" Commander Dragonfly shouted over her helmet comm.

"We'll be there in 10," Lt Locust replied.

"Make it sooner." Dragonfly ordered.

"I can feel the newborns coming," Dr Leialoha warned. She looked down at the still-oozing wound on her tentacle. "And I don't think they'll hesitate to eat their own kind."

"Bug Team! Defensive perimeter!" Dragonfly barked.

The team lined up between the archaeologists and the oncoming threat. They raised their weapons, ready to fire. Dr Leialoha did not protest. As the commander awaited the assault, and the ship, she noticed a herd of grazing beasts visible in the meadow beyond the trees. They looked like the same ones that had stampeded through the camp earlier, but now they had Medusa tentacles. The sight gave her an idea.

"Maybe we won't be on the menu after all," Dragonfly said, and then called the ship on her comm. "*Arion*, buzz that herd in the meadow. Send them towards us in the forest."

A few moments later the sound of the *Arion*'s engines roared above them. The ship swooped towards the grazing beasts. The animals stampeded towards the forest as the first wave of larval Medusas confronted the Bug Team.

"Head for the herd. They're the meal you're looking for," Dragonfly muttered, as if willing the newborns to turn. She did not drop her aim.

Suddenly, the larval horde noticed the herding beasts and rushed off in the direction of the larger, more plentiful food source.

"The grazing animals are part of the plan!" Leialoha suddenly realized as another Medusa memory came into her mind. "The newborns need those large herds to eat, not small birds or insects. Now I understand the food chain on this planet."

"We might have escaped being the first course, but we aren't sticking around to be the second," Dragonfly declared.

The Bug Team maintained their defensive position while the *Arion* landed. The archaeologists scrambled aboard. No one relaxed until the ship was in orbit.

"I wouldn't mind going back," Dr Leialoha told Commander Dragonfly later.

"We just escaped with our lives," Dragonfly reminded the archaeologist.

"Call it scientific curiosity," Leialoha shrugged. "I want to watch the progress of a resurrected species. I might even stay half-Medusa for a while. I have some of their memories, and it helps me to identify with them."

"Are you sure? With Dr Barrington working on the reversal of the Medusa implant tech and the skill of Coalition genetic surgeons, you and your colleagues can likely be restored to human form," Commander Dragonfly observed.

Leialoha studied the half-human, half-insect form of Bug Team Alpha's commanding officer.

"Yes, I'm sure. After all, being half bug has worked just fine for you," Leialoha observed.

"You'll get no argument from me," Dragonfly replied with a smile.

Mission report

TOP SECRET AND CONFIDENTIAL

TO: GENERAL JAMES CLAUDIUS BARRETT, COMMANDER OF COLONIAL ARMED FORCES

FROM: COMMANDER ARIEL "DRAGONFLY" CARTER, BUG TEAM ALPHA

SUBJECT: NIBURI 3 ARCHAEOLOGICAL DIG RESCUE

MISSION DETAILS:

Mission Planet: Niburi 3
Mission Parameters: Search and rescue
Mission Team: Bug Team Alpha [BTA]
* Commander Ariel "Dragonfly" Carter
* Lt Liu "Hopper" Yu
* Lt Akiko "Radar" Murasaki
* Lt Irene "Impact" Mallory
* Lt Gustav "Burrow" Von Braun
* Lt Sancho "Locust" Castillo

MISSION SUMMARY:

Archaeological project known as the "Medusa Dig" attacked by unknown hostile entity or entities; one project member missing.

Upon arrival on Niburi 3, BTA was met by dig project leader Dr Astrid Leialoha. En route to the dig site, BTA and Leialoha were informed that a hostile had been captured and confined. Examination of the hostile led to the conclusion that it was a living example of the planet's extinct civilization known as the "Medusas."

During the initial search for the missing project member, BTA encountered a second hostile. This resulted in the discovery of an unknown burial tomb and mummies. Further search led to a deeper chamber where BTA and Dr Leialoha were attacked by a swarm of Medusa DNA drones. A drone implanted a device in Leialoha that initiated a transformation from human to Medusa. A drone attack on the rest of the dig personnel resulted in a total of 12 people becoming the victims of Medusa transformation.

An immediate evacuation was ordered to protect the remaining personnel. BTA tracked the transformed personnel to the drone chamber, where they were producing larval Medusa life forms. This was later determined to be a resurrection protocol put in place by the earlier civilization prior to its extinction. All Medusa Dig Project personnel were successfully evacuated from Niburi 3. Genetic reversal of Medusa DNA is currently in progress. Dr Leialoha has opted to delay genetic reversal at this time.

APPENDIX 1: TRANSPORT
1 spacecraft: Zip-Class, *Arion*; 2 Hover Hogs; 1 Bug Bike

APPENDIX 2: ADDITIONAL PARTICIPANTS
24 archaeologists, including:
Dr Astrid Leialoha, Medusa dig project leader
Dr Michael Barrington, project field physician
Dr Millerd Franks, project archaeologist
Dr Laurel Franks, project archaeologist

END REPORT

Glossary

DNA molecule that carries all of the instructions to make a living thing and keep it working; DNA is short for deoxyribonucleic acid

drone unmanned, remote-controlled device

genetic relating to physical traits or conditions passed down from parents to children

larval relating to the immature young of an insect or other animal

Medusa female monster from Greek mythology with wings and snakes for hair

polycrete very strong cement used in buildings

reanimate come to life again

schematic relating to a plan, map or scheme

tendril long, thin, curling appendage that helps animals attach to and climb up things

xenoform strange or alien body or being

About the author

Laurie S Sutton has been interested in science fiction ever since she first saw the *Sputnik* satellite speed across the night sky as a very young child. By 12 years old, she was reading books by classic sci-fi authors Robert Heinlein, Isaac Azimov and Arthur C Clarke. Then she discovered *STAR TREK*.

Laurie's love of outer space has led her to write *STAR TREK* comics for *DC* Comics, *Malibu* Comics and *Marvel* Comics. From her home in Florida, USA, she has watched many Space Shuttle launches blaze a trail though the sky. Now she watches the night sky as the International Space Station sails overhead instead of *Sputnik*.

About the illustrator

James Nathaniel is a digital comic book artist and illustrator from the UK. With a graphics tablet and pen, he produces dramatic narrative-focused fantasy, science fiction and non-fiction work. His work is the result of inspiration accumulated from the likes of Sean Gordon Murphy, Jake Wyatt, Jamie Hewlett and Jon Foster, as well as many years playing video games and watching films. In the near future, James hopes to write and illustrate his own graphic novels from stories he's been developing over the years.

Discussion questions

1. How do you think the Franks transformed into Medusas? Was it similar to what happened to the archaeologists later in the story? Explain your answer.

2. Did the Medusas need the help of the archaeologists to resurrect their species? Explain your answer.

3. Do you think Dr Leialoha and the other archaeologists made the right decision to leave Niburi 3 with Bug Team Alpha on the *Arion*? Explain why or why not.

Writing prompts

1. Imagine you were a member of Bug Team Alpha. What bug or insect would you model your new body after? Using descriptive language, write about what physical features and elite fighting skills you would have.

2. Commander Dragonfly's mission to rescue and evacuate the archaeologists conflicted at times with Dr Leialoha and her team's mission. Write about a time you disagreed with someone about the best thing to do in a certain situation. What was ultimately decided? How did you come to this conclusion?

3. What happens next in the story? You decide! Write a chapter about what happens after the *Arion* returns to Earth. Will the Bug Team members be sent on a new mission? What happens to the archaeologists who turned into Medusas? Will Dr Leialoha go back to Niburi 3?

BUG TEAM ALPHA

BUG TEAM ALPHA

THE DIG

When an archaeologist goes missing and presumed kidnapped during an expedition, Bug Team Alpha is called in to help.

BUG TEAM ALPHA

THE DRACO

The president of Earth has been kidnapped by Draco warrior forces. Can Bug Team Alpha rescue her in time?

BUG TEAM ALPHA

INVISIBLE ENEMY

Talos is under attack, but no one can see exactly who - or what - the enemy is. Bug Team Alpha is called in to fight.

BUG TEAM ALPHA

STRANDED

What happens when Bug Team Alpha's transport ship crash lands after intersecting an interplanetary war zone? Read *Stranded* to find out!